TREASURE QUEST

"What does it say, Gamell?" Tag asked eagerly.

"It happens to be a ship's manifest. A ship called *El Patrón*."

"I don't get it—" Cowboy started.

Tag held up his hand to silence his friend. "Let Gamell finish."

The old man cleared his throat. "*El Patrón* was a galleon on its way back to Spain from a trade mission. It went down in a hurricane and most of the crew and passengers were lost. A few members of the crew escaped with this. This manifest is now more than three hundred years old. It lists the silver, gold, and other cargo that was aboard *El Patrón*." He took a second yellowed piece of paper out of the case. "This is another account of the cargo. The unregistered cargo, that is. It's signed by an Admiral Bartolomé de Campos, who survived the shipwreck."

"Shipwreck?" Tag said the word almost reverently.

"The one your daddy was looking for, Tag."

OTHER YEARLING BOOKS YOU WILL ENJOY:

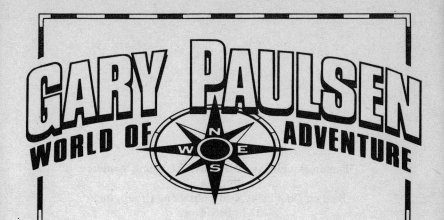

THE
TREASURE OF
EL PATRÓN

A YEARLING BOOK

Published by
Bantam Doubleday Dell Books for Young Readers
a division of
Bantam Doubleday Dell Publishing Group, Inc.
1540 Broadway
New York, New York 10036

The trademarks Yearling® and Dell® are registered in the
U.S. Patent and Trademark Office and in other countries.

ISBN: 0-440-41048-7

Series design: Barbara Berger

Interior illustration by Michael David Biegel

Printed in the United States of America

April 1996

OPM 10 9 8 7 6 5 4 3 2 1

Dear Readers:

Real adventure is many things—it's danger and daring and sometimes even a struggle for life or death. From competing in the Iditarod dogsled race across Alaska to sailing the Pacific Ocean, I've experienced some of this adventure myself. I try to capture this spirit in my stories, and each time I sit down to write, that challenge is a bit of an adventure in itself.

You're all a part of this adventure as well. Over the years I've had the privilege of talking with many of you in schools, and this book is the result of hearing firsthand what you want to read about most—power-packed action and excitement.

You asked for it—so hang on tight while we jump into another thrilling story in my World of Adventure.

Gary Paulsen

THE
TREASURE OF
EL PATRÓN

1641

Admiral Bartolomé de Campos of the Spanish galleon *El Patrón* set his jaw and stared grimly at the vast horizon.

The wind was beginning to die.

He'd seen it like this only a few times before. The air was thick with a muggy yellow haze, and in the distance high, thin clouds rolled across the sky.

It was coming. He could smell it. Why wouldn't that fool Captain Vargas pay attention to him and ready for bad weather?

The admiral considered their vessel. *El Patrón* was a top-heavy, leaky ship that seemed to require constant manning of her pumps just to keep her afloat.

The ship was overloaded in every way—a fact the admiral had complained about also, but to no avail. Some 495 passengers and more than 140 tons of cargo took up practically every square inch of room.

It was the cargo the admiral thought of now. There was, of course, the consignment of gold and silver belonging to the Spanish Crown. And there were the Chinese porcelain and silks brought aboard to use for trading purposes in the colonies.

But there was also the contraband, large fortunes in gold bars accumulated by colonial traders and smuggled aboard ship by bribing the officers to not declare it on the manifest. In addition there were the personal items, jewelry and precious gems of great value that the more important passengers had managed to conceal and bring aboard.

The admiral thought of his own personal contraband. He was fond of one item in particular—a gold dagger with three perfect emeralds in the hilt, given to him in the colonies by a very special lady.

The wind suddenly picked up. Whitecaps appeared on the surface of the ocean and rain began pelting the deck. The admiral raced to speak to the pilot.

The galleon was already being tossed about like a child's toy. From somewhere forward, timbers snapped. To lighten the ship, the frantic crew began tossing the deck cargo overboard, along with five of the ship's bronze cannons.

In the first hour of the hurricane, the mainmast was cut in two. As it fell into the ocean it took with it immense portions of rigging. *El Patrón* was crippled and water was coming in faster than the crew could pump it out.

The struggle lasted three days. Miraculously, *El Patrón* stayed afloat. Some of the crew and passengers had been lost, but those remaining had worked around the clock to hold the water at bay, while others had managed to rig a makeshift sail.

They had been blown so far off course that the captain and pilots were confused about their position. To the admiral, however, the new area seemed familiar. He was convinced they were near the deadly coral reefs that extended some twelve miles off Bermuda in the western North Atlantic Ocean.

His suspicions were proved correct late that third night. It was midnight when the galleon struck a reef, and with a sickening crunch the ship lurched to one side. It jolted to a stop and then pitched forward, the hull scraping against a rock. Water began gushing in.

The crew manned the longboats, forgetting their duties and leaving most of the passengers, including the Archbishop of Havana, to a watery grave. The brave admiral elected to go down with his ship. But as the galleon heaved and the bow rose, he was flung into the foamy black sea. Sailors from a departing longboat hoisted him, barely breathing, aboard and set out in the darkness.

CHAPTER 1

"Hey, wake up, mate. Maybe I want to buy something here."

Thirteen-year-old Tag Jones's eyes flew open. He scrambled to an upright position from his makeshift bed on the bright pink Bermuda sand inside the bait shack. "I'm awake, I—Cowboy! I ought to—"

"Ought to thank me, that's what." The tall, dark native Bermudian boy folded his arms smugly.

Tag scowled at his friend. "For what? Waking me out of one of the best dreams I ever had?"

"I got something better than an old day-dream about Spanish gold. I got tourists."

"Where?" Tag jumped up, leaned over the bait shop counter, and searched the narrow strip of beach. "I don't see anybody."

Cowboy, whose real name was Kevin Trace, whipped the tattered straw hat that had earned him his nickname off his head in exasperation. "I didn't bring them with me, mate. They asked where was a good place to get fishing equipment and bait. I gave directions to your shack here on the beach and then hurried up here to tell you. Besides, I figure you don't want to be caught sleeping by a couple of rich tourists."

Tag stretched and ran his hand through his sandy brown hair. "What makes you think they're rich?"

Cowboy grinned. "I been following them for a while. They're handing out money right and left."

Tag's face brightened. He fingered the worn Spanish coin that hung on a chain around his neck. "Maybe we'll get enough to get my reserve tank fixed and we can go down again."

"Shooo. Is that all you think about? Diving by those reefs? There ain't nothing down there. Every treasure hunter on these islands done been all over them reefs. Nobody ever come up with nothing."

"Then where did this come from?" Tag held out the gold coin.

"Your daddy was one of the best divers around here. He gave that piece to you before he died. And I know all about his diary telling how he thinks there's more where that come from. But if he were here right now, he'd tell you he didn't know for sure."

"He knew." Tag pulled a T-shirt over his deeply tanned upper body.

The sound of two approaching mopeds interrupted their conversation. Cowboy wisely stepped around the corner of the small thatched building, out of sight. He didn't want the potential customers to think he had been scamming them.

The men were tourists. That was easy to spot. But there was something about them that made Tag uneasy.

The taller man wore his blond hair pulled

straight back in a tight, greasy ponytail. His eyes looked over a sharp nose in an icy blue stare. The other man had a shiny bald head. He was shorter and heavier and did most of the talking.

"My friend and I are interested in renting some equipment to go fishing."

Tag nodded. "Sure thing. What are you going after?"

The man hesitated. "Does it matter? We just want to fish. You set us up and we'll pay you and be on our way."

Tag scratched his head. "Are you going to be close to shore or out in deep sea?"

"Why do you want to know?" the tall man growled.

The bald man put up his hand. "It's all right, Spear, the kid asked a perfectly logical question." He turned to Tag. "We thought we'd go out in the bay a ways. Maybe fish around the reefs some. You have any suggestions?"

Normally Tag would have given them some advice, but the way the blond man spoke made him uncomfortable. "I hear they're having some luck out in the harbor." Tag gathered up two long, thin poles and bagged some bait. Then he set a rental agreement on the counter. "Sign here, mister. Oh, and you need to have the poles back by this time tomorrow."

The heavyset man signed the slip, paid him, and gave him a generous twenty-dollar tip. "Thanks a lot, kid. We'll see you tomorrow afternoon."

Cowboy stepped back into the shack and the two boys watched the men drive away. "You made a killing, mate. And on top of that, they're coming back tomorrow."

Tag split the tip with his friend. "There's something wrong with those guys. They didn't know the first thing about fishing."

"Who cares? They're probably just tourists who want to brag to their friends back home. Besides, they pay good."

Tag shrugged. "You have a point there. What do you say we close up shop and go into town and get that tank of mine fixed?"

"Now you're talking."

CHAPTER 2

 The road into town was crowded with slow-moving taxicabs, mopeds, bicycles, and colorfully dressed pedestrians. The native Bermudians were either related to or knew everyone in the village. They waved and smiled at the boys.

A tall, muscular policeman dressed in military-style shorts, which exposed a long, puckered scar on his right leg, stood in the center of the street directing traffic. He stopped the oncoming cars and motioned for the boys to cross. "How's your mama, Tag?"

"She's fine, Thomas."

The officer raised one eyebrow and slowly

limped across the street with them. "Some saying maybe she works too hard down at that tourist café."

Tag smiled at the man, who had been one of his father's closest friends. "*Some* would probably know. See you around, Thomas."

Thomas winked at Cowboy. "You try and keep this no-account white boy out of trouble, hear?"

"It'll be hard, but I'll try." Cowboy ran to catch up with Tag. "Want me to carry your tank?"

"No thanks, I've got it. Come on, we better hustle if we're gonna catch Gamell before he closes."

Tag led the way to the other side of town and up a steep road to a small, run-down shop with a sign above the door that said DIVING.

A small silver bell tinkled as they burst through the screen door. An old man with wrinkled grayish black skin and streaks of white in his hair looked up and smiled, showing that he was missing two front teeth. "Tag, boy. What do you know?"

"I need you to look at my tank if you have time, Gamell."

The elderly man put on his glasses and examined the tank in silence. He tapped the gauge. "Here's your problem. I'll have it fixed in no time." He took it apart and began replacing fittings. "You boys going down this evening?"

Tag nodded. "Thought we'd take another look at Tiger Head reef."

Gamell shook his head. "Just like your daddy. Always searching for the big treasure."

"It's out there, Gamell, and I'm gonna be the one to bring it in."

Gamell studied the boy with sharp eyes. "I was hoping you would eventually give it up. But I can see you won't ever quit until you find it." The old man blew air through the gap between his teeth. "Maybe it's time I showed you something." He shuffled out of the room and returned in a few moments with a polished wooden case. He took a rolled-up piece of paper out of it. Gently he slid a faded red ribbon off the document and slowly spread the paper out on the counter.

The boys crowded in for a closer look. It was a list written in Spanish.

"What does it say, Gamell?" Tag asked eagerly.

"It happens to be a ship's manifest. A ship called *El Patrón.*"

"I don't get it—" Cowboy started.

Tag held up his hand to silence his friend. "Let Gamell finish."

The old man cleared his throat. "*El Patrón* was a galleon on its way back to Spain from a trade mission. It went down in a hurricane and most of the crew and passengers were lost. A few members of the crew escaped with this. This manifest is now more than three hundred years old. It lists the silver, gold and other cargo that was aboard *El Patrón.*" He took a second yellowed piece of paper out of the case. "This is another account of the cargo. The unregistered cargo, that is. It's signed by an Admiral Bartolomé de Campos, who survived the shipwreck."

"Shipwreck?" Tag said the word almost reverently.

"The one your daddy was looking for, Tag."

"You know where it is, Gamell?"

"Not the exact location. All I have is the admiral's account, which is not too specific.

14

Here; it's somewhere under this reef." He pointed at a map taped to the counter. "That's where your father thought it was."

The old man grew solemn and rolled up the paper. "I showed this manifest to your daddy and it was the cause of his death. Thomas lost his job as chief of police because of his hurt leg. I wouldn't be showing it to you now except I know you're hardheaded and not going to stop no matter what."

"My father was killed in a diving accident, Gamell. His regulator malfunctioned at the bottom of the ocean. Thomas tried to save him and lost part of his leg to a barracuda. It wasn't your fault. No one could have done anything."

"It could be the treasure." Gamell looked at Tag sadly. "The ones who practice bush, bad magic, call it cursed. No one else from the island would even think of looking for it."

"Bush." Tag spit on the floor. "You believe in that voodoo junk?"

Gamell studied the boy again. "Maybe. But who knows, Tag. Could be you're just the one to break the spell."

Chapter 3

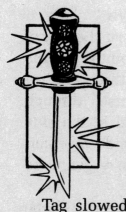

"Look who's coming." Cowboy pointed to a blue-and-white outboard headed toward them on the bay. "It's those tourists who rented poles from you earlier."

Tag slowed their boat and waited for the two men to get closer. "Have any luck?" he yelled.

The one called Spear glared at him. The bald man, who had signed his name on the rental agreement as George Davis, waved. "No luck at all, kid. We're gonna call it a day." He stared at Cowboy. "Don't I know you?" Without waiting for an answer, he continued.

"Where are you two headed? Getting a little late for fishing, isn't it? It's almost dark."

"Going out to practice some night diving."

"Diving? For what?" the man asked.

Tag shrugged. "Nothing in particular. Just diving." Not wanting to tell them his plans, he gunned the motor and yelled over the noise, "See you around, Mr. Davis."

When they reached the spot near the end of the reef that Gamell had pinpointed on the map, Tag killed the engine and threw the anchor overboard. Excitement coursed through him as the gentle waves lapped at the side of the boat. He rubbed his hands together. "This is it, Cowboy. Tonight we're gonna be rich!"

Cowboy slid his tank over his head. "I hope you're right. I sure wouldn't mind letting someone else clean those fish down at the market."

Tag already had his equipment on. He handed Cowboy his extra waterproof flashlight, stuck a Ping-Pong paddle in his weight belt, and gave the thumbs-down sign to go over the edge. Cowboy returned the signal and they rolled backward into the water.

The trip to the bottom was executed in a thick blackness. Tag exhaled, and as his lungs emptied he began to sink farther into the chilly water. Pain shot into his left ear. *Stupid,* he thought. *A first-year diver knows you have to relieve the pressure.* With all the excitement, he had forgotten. Quickly he pinched his nose and blew out.

In a little less than a minute they were on the sandy bottom. Cowboy pointed his light at the red-and-orange coral. A school of yellowtail snapper swam by in front of him.

Tag tapped his friend on the shoulder and pointed to the right. Cowboy nodded. He understood that they had less than an hour's worth of air and that they would have to split up if they hoped to find any trace of the treasure.

Almost thirty minutes had passed before Tag saw anything that caught his attention. He'd been in this area before but somehow he'd missed this. It was a small round opening the size of a plate near the bottom of the reef.

Tag pointed his light at the hole and peered inside. How could he not have seen it before?

The inside was hollow, like an underwater cave. Something shiny lay near the opening and reflected the beam from his flashlight. He reached inside and pulled it out.

A pewter spoon.

If he could have, he would have screamed with joy. He tucked the spoon into his vest pocket and reached into the hole again. This time he used the Ping-Pong paddle to delicately sweep the sand from the floor of the cave. As if by magic, a plate and knife appeared. Tag put the paddle back in his belt and reached for the two new treasures.

A sharp stab of pain shot through his left hand. Something had hold of the tip of his thumb and was trying to yank him into the hole.

The flesh ripped from the end of Tag's thumb. A small moray eel gulped it down and then released its grip to try to get a better hold on the rest of his finger.

Tag jerked his arm out and swam back from the hole. The pain was worse than a thousand sharp needles all jabbed into his hand at once. A greenish fluid surged from the end of his thumb. Tag knew it was the color of his own blood under the water. He held the wound and tried to keep from passing out.

Frantically he searched for Cowboy. When he spotted him he gave the sign to go up and tried not to panic as he headed for the surface. It was all he could do to resist the urge to shoot to the top. *Stay calm,* he told himself. *Breathe deeply and don't rise any higher than the air bubbles from your tank.* Tag knew that if he went up too fast he might get the bends and become paralyzed, or die.

In the boat, Cowboy helped him lift his tank off his back, then whipped off his own tank. "What happened down there?"

Tag showed him his thumb. "Nearly lost it to a bloody moray."

"That's it." Cowboy threw his hands up in disgust. "No more night diving for us. Anything we want to see we'll just have to find in the daytime." He flipped open the first-aid kit and grabbed a roll of bandages.

"Take a look at this." With his good hand, Tag pulled the antique spoon out of his pocket and held it up. "Thanks to Gamell's maps and the old admiral's records, I think we may have found the hiding place of *El Patrón.*"

CHAPTER 4

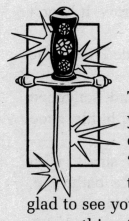

Tag opened the gate to his back-yard and stepped in. A big ball of white fur hit him in the chest. "Hey, watch it, Ghost!" Tag patted his big, shaggy mutt. "I'm glad to see you too, boy. You been keeping an eye on things?" The dog whined and wagged his tail vigorously.

Tag glanced at Cowboy. "Want to come in for a while?"

Cowboy set his tank next to the compressor on Tag's back porch. "No, I better get home, mate. It's getting late. My dad'll be having fits."

"Okay. I'll see you tomorrow, then. Come by the bait shack when you get the day's catch cleaned. Maybe we can close up early and get started looking for the treasure."

"We're going down tomorrow?" Cowboy raised one eyebrow and pointed to his friend's thumb. "What about that?"

"Aw, it's nothing. By tomorrow it won't even hurt."

"If you say so." Cowboy bounded down the steps. "See ya."

Tag waved goodbye to his friend, scratched Ghost's ears one more time with his good hand, and went inside.

The white-roofed house was small, with only two bedrooms, a kitchen, a bathroom, and a tiny living room. The lights were out, which meant his mother still wasn't home from work. Not that he expected her. During the summer months she always worked late.

He flipped on the light switch in the kitchen and headed for the refrigerator. Careful not to touch anything with his injured thumb, he pulled out some leftover fish chowder and heated it on the stove.

When he had finished eating, Tag cleaned up his mess and settled down on the worn, overstuffed couch with his father's diary and the spoon he'd found.

The diary was precious to him. He'd found it in his dad's gear after his dad had died, and had never shown it to anyone. The only person he'd ever told about it was Cowboy. He especially didn't want to tell his mother because she worried enough about his "preoccupation" with his dad's last dive.

It wasn't written like most diaries, in which routine daily events were recorded. This one was a log of "finds."

Since before Tag was born in Bermuda's Smith's parish, his father had always worked for someone else, going on whatever diving expedition paid the most money. On his final dive, he and his good friend Thomas had worked as partners, searching for their own lost treasure.

Normally Tag loved to pore over descriptions of the salvage operations, imagining what it must have been like to work with so many diving crews, searching through old wrecks for buried treasure. But this time he skipped to the end of the entries.

June 17—Thomas and I are getting close. Found only one gold coin—hole reef—but am sure more will follow.

Tag's mouth fell open. It had been right there all the time and he'd missed it. His dad had left him a clue, *hole reef*. Before, because the diary was so water-damaged and words and letters were smeared or missing, he'd thought the entry said there was only one coin on the *whole* reef. But his father had been talking about the exact same place Tag and Cowboy had been today—a small round *hole* in the side of the reef.

So they *had* found it.

But now what? If the reef had grown over the wreck, how would they ever get to it?

Tag's thoughts were interrupted by the sound of the front door closing. He slid the diary and spoon under a couch cushion and jumped up to help his mother with the heavy sack she was carrying.

She gratefully handed it to him while she

kicked off her shoes and pulled the scarf out of her long, blond hair. "Harry down at the café sent you some of his cassava pie and . . . Tag?"

Tag stopped halfway to the kitchen and turned. His mother's blue eyes looked worried.

"What happened to your thumb?" She pointed at the bloodstain on the white bandage.

"Oh, that. It's no big deal. Cowboy and I were diving off the Tiger Head and I ran into a little trouble with a moray."

His mother dropped wearily into a nearby chair. "The Tiger Head? That's where your father . . ." Her voice trailed off.

Tag put the sack on a low table and walked over to her. "I was careful, Mom. Cowboy and I aren't exactly amateurs, you know."

"Neither was your father . . . or Thomas. I know I can't ask you to stop diving. It's in your blood. But couldn't you at least choose another place?"

Tag hated to see her upset. He knelt by her chair and decided it would be in everyone's best interests for him to stretch the truth a little. "Don't worry about it, okay? One place is as good as the next as far as I'm concerned."

Relief washed over her face. "Good. Want me to take a look at that thumb?"

Tag shook his head. "It was just a little nip. Cowboy cleaned it up real good. It'll be good as new by morning." He stood and moved to the sack. "Now, weren't you saying something about cassava pie?"

CHAPTER 5

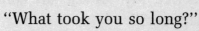

"What took you so long?"

"Long?" Cowboy tried to look offended. "So that's the thanks I get for working my tail off just so you can hurry over to Tiger Head and be live bait for some hungry moray."

"Very funny. Besides, that's not going to happen this time." Tag held up two large salted fish. "These are my insurance. The first one is for the moray that nipped my thumb yesterday. I'm bringing the second in case he has any friends living down there with him."

"So what are we waiting on? Let's get going."

"I can't. Your tourists still haven't brought my poles back."

"*My* tourists?"

"You remember, those two guys you sent here who didn't know anything about fishing, Davis and Spear."

"I remember, but—" Cowboy broke off as they heard the sound of a moped engine. "Looks like 'my' tourists are coming. Want me to disappear?"

"No. They saw you in the boat with me last night. Anyway, as soon as I get the poles, we're out of here."

Only one moped pulled up to the bait shack. This time Davis was alone. The stocky man passed the poles to Tag and waited while the boy put them away.

"Is there something else I can help you with, Mr. Davis?"

"As a matter of fact, I was wondering if you boys might be able to do something for me. Yesterday, when my friend and I were out near the reefs, we accidentally dropped something in the water. Since neither one of us dives, I was hoping I could hire you to find it for me."

Tag rubbed the back of his neck. "I don't know. We sort of had other plans for today."

"Excuse us a minute." Cowboy took his friend's arm and propelled him to the back of the shack. "We're going down there anyway, right?" he whispered.

"Right."

"Why not make a little money while we're at it?"

"We won't need any money if I can figure out how to get to that wreck."

Cowboy sighed. "Okay, then let me make the money while you look for the treasure."

"Have it your way. But you have to get rid of them as soon as you find their stuff."

"No problem." Cowboy moved to the counter. "My friend and I would be happy to dive for you, Mr. Davis."

CHAPTER 6

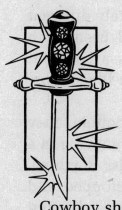

Tag steered his boat in the wake of the blue-and-white outboard directly in front of him. "Did those guys tell you what they dropped?"

Cowboy shook his head. "Davis said it was extremely valuable and he'd rather not say what it was. We're supposed to recognize it because it's wrapped in a yellow plastic bag. He's already given me a deposit. If we find it, he'll give us more."

"The sooner we find it the better. Those two guys are weird, if you ask me. Why wouldn't they want us to know what's in the bag?"

Davis and Spear stopped near the edge of the reef. Tag anchored a few yards away. Davis cupped his hands and yelled, "We think it's somewhere around here." He pointed to the area in front of his boat.

Tag and Cowboy checked their equipment and rolled over the side of the boat into the ocean. The water looked completely different in the daylight. At night it had been pitch black and ominous; now it was a beautiful clear blue. The sand was a pale bluish gray and the fish were bluish green.

When the boys reached the bottom, they searched the left side of the reef, moving in a zigzag so that they wouldn't miss anything. Near the end of the reef Tag stopped and looked for the small hole where he'd found his treasures the night before. He swam by it twice, wishing they hadn't agreed to dive for Davis and Spear.

Tag moved to Cowboy and tapped him on the shoulder, shrugged, and gave the thumbs-up sign. Cowboy followed him to the top.

They surfaced near the left side of Davis's boat. The bald man leaned over. Beads of sweat clung to his head. "Did you find it?"

"We searched this whole side carefully. There's nothing here."

Spear slammed the side of the boat with his fist. "I told you we shouldn't have hired kids," he said angrily.

"Shut up." Davis turned to the boys and mopped his forehead with his shirtsleeve. "Perhaps we made a mistake about the location. It's hard to be sure out here. Everything looks the same. Would you mind looking around the other side?"

Tag rolled his eyes. He wanted these people gone so that he could get back to the treasure.

Davis pulled out his wallet. "There'll be a bonus in it for you. Say . . . fifty bucks apiece."

Tag looked at his friend. Cowboy's eyes were pleading with him to say yes.

"Oh, all right. We'll go down again. But this is the last time."

They swam to their own boat, changed to their reserve air tanks, then dropped back to the bottom. Halfway around the reef they both spotted it at the same time. The mystery package was wrapped in yellow plastic as Davis had said. But something was attached to it.

Tag lifted it a few feet off the bottom. Sand drifted up and clouded his vision. When it was clear he could see that a deflated rubber buoy was attached to the yellow package with heavy string.

Cowboy took one side of the package and gave the sign to go up. Tag shook his head. He didn't want to give them the bundle until he knew what was in it. From the looks of it, it had been dropped in the water on purpose, not accidentally.

He put his hand out, palm down, and rocked it back and forth, giving his friend the sign that meant *something is wrong.* Then he put both his fists up, indicating that he wanted Cowboy to wait.

Tag wrapped the buoy around the yellow package, swam across the reef to his treasure hole, and dropped it inside. Then he went back to his friend and gave the thumbs-up sign.

Through the water they could see the bottom of their boat. But they could see something else too: a grayish blur a few yards out in front of it.

A tiger shark.

The twelve-foot creature opened its mouth, exposing rows of saw-edged teeth as it swam in a wide circle around the two boats. One unblinking dark eye seemed to be looking at them but paid no real attention.

They knew better than to surface. The shark might think they were fish in trouble.

Suddenly the shark began thrashing and rolling in the water. Streaks of green spurted from its body.

Tag pointed up and both boys surfaced and climbed into the boat as quickly as possible.

Spear was standing near the edge of his boat with a handgun pointed at the water. He yelled over at them, "Saved your lives, squirts! You should thank me."

"Nearly got us killed, you mean." Tag was furious. He slipped his tank off his back. "In a few minutes, every shark within miles will be here to help finish him off. Watch this." He picked up one of his salted fish and threw it out into the water. The ocean boiled furiously. Two or three fins were plainly visible.

A large shark took a bite out of the smaller one that had downed the fish.

"Diving's over, Mr. Davis. It'll be hours before their feeding frenzy ends. Besides, there's nothing down there."

Davis studied Tag's face. "We'll just have to see about that, son."

CHAPTER 7

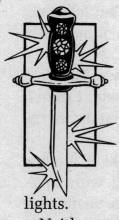

Later that night, under cover of
darkness, two figures hoisted a
bundle wrapped up in yellow
plastic into their boat and sped
toward shore without using any
lights.

Neither one uttered a word as they secured
the small boat to an old makeshift dock and
hurried across the beach and up a rocky trail
toward an abandoned lighthouse.

Tag closed the creaky door of the lighthouse
and snapped on a small flashlight. "All right.
Let's see what's so important to those two
guys."

Cowboy cut the string from the buoy with his diving knife and pulled it away from the package. Then he made a careful incision near the top of the yellow plastic and pulled out a small, clear plastic bag containing white powder.

Tag turned the yellow package over and dumped the rest of its contents. Out fell nine more small bags. Each one was filled with powder.

They sat quietly for a while. It was Cowboy who broke the silence. "Sorry, mate. I didn't know they were dope dealers. What do we do now?"

Tag rubbed his chin. "This looks like a big haul. I don't think we're dealing with amateurs here. My guess is someone made the drop from the air and Spear and Davis were supposed to pick it up. But somehow the buoy got a hole in it and the whole package sank to the bottom."

"Do we take it to the police?"

"That's the tricky part. It's hard to make a move on this island without everybody and their grandmother knowing about it. These kinds of people are mean, and if we don't want their buddies coming after us, we're gonna have to be real careful."

"I've got it." Cowboy started stuffing the bags back into the large yellow container. "We'll put it all back where it came from and nobody will be the wiser."

Tag looked at him.

Cowboy made a face. "Okay, so that was a bad idea. You have a better one?"

"No. But I know who will—Thomas." Tag helped stuff the rest of the bags inside the larger one. "Help me hide this and let's get the boat back to the marina. Tomorrow we'll show Thomas what we've got and let him decide what to do."

They hid the bag in a corner of the closet under the stairs and crept out to the boat. Tag rounded the tip of the island and expertly maneuvered the small craft through the reefs to the marina.

"I'll meet you at the bait shack tomorrow afternoon," he whispered. "We'll go into town together."

As the boys split up and hurried away, a

man stepped from behind one of the gas pumps on the dock. He flicked a cigarette butt into the water. His eyes narrowed as he quietly made his way back up the beach to the motel.

Chapter 8

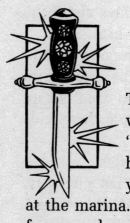

The sun was just coming up when Tag locked the back gate. "Sorry, Ghost. You have to stay here. Can't have a monster like you running around loose down at the marina." He put his hand through the fence and scratched behind his pet's big, floppy ears. Then he turned and ran down the road past the dock and up the beach to the bait shack.

The door to the shack was hanging by one hinge. It had been kicked in. The counter was on its side and all the bait had been dumped in a pile on the floor. On top of the pile was a crude homemade doll with sandy brown hair. A hatpin was stuck through its middle.

"Looks like somebody don't like you much, mate."

Tag whirled around. An older boy with ebony skin, a scar under one eye, and muscles bulging through his ragged shirt stood in the doorway laughing. Two other boys about the same age and size were behind him.

Tag had seen them before, hanging around over on St. David's Island. The people up there were a close-knit group and usually kept to themselves, so he didn't know these kids by name.

"Did you do this?" he demanded.

The big boy laughed harder. "Let's just say, the boss man, he don't like no double-cross."

"What are you talking about?"

"The boss man says if he finds out you're holding out on him, he's gonna come visit you and your mama in the middle of the night."

Tag clenched his fists. He rushed forward in a rage, but the older boy was ready. He punched Tag hard in the stomach, knocking him to the ground. Tag gasped for air and crawled to his knees. He heard a click of metal.

The other boy had a switchblade.

Tag scrambled backward. The boy stepped menacingly toward him, waving the knife in his face.

"What's going on here?"

Thomas was standing in the doorway. Tag had never been so glad to see anyone in his life.

The boy closed the knife and slid it into his pocket before Thomas could see it. He turned to face the police officer. "No trouble here, man." The three older boys moved around Thomas to the door.

The leader stopped. "By the way, little man," he said to Tag, "the boss man hired him some real divers. Not scrap salvers, like you and your friend. He says you better hope they don't come up empty." The older boy's eyes held a warning. "He also says to watch your mouth . . . or else."

CHAPTER 9

Thomas helped Tag to his feet. His trained eyes surveyed the damage in the room. "Did those hoodlums do this? I can have them picked up before they get across town."

Tag shook his head. "I'd rather you didn't."

"Somehow I figured you would say that." Thomas picked up the straw doll. "Bush? Are you into something over your head, son?"

"I . . . I can't talk about it right now. I need time to think about all this, Thomas."

Thomas sat on the edge of the overturned counter. "Word is that you've been working for some pretty tough-looking characters. That's why I'm here."

"Have you been spying on me?"

"No need to. Not much that happens on this island gets past the gossip chain. You know that. Want to tell me about it?"

More than anything Tag longed to tell his father's friend about the contents of the yellow package. But he remembered the threat the older boy had made against his mother and decided to wait. "There's nothing to tell."

Thomas put his hand on the boy's shoulder. "These kinds of people are serious, Tag. They're not playing games."

"I can take care of myself."

"So I see." Thomas looked around the ransacked room, handed Tag the voodoo doll, and stood up. "I can't make you tell me, Tag. But if you need me, call day or night. I'll come." The tall man limped to the door.

"Thomas?"

The officer turned and waited patiently.

Tag gulped. "Thanks. I mean for helping me out just now. I guess I was in a tight spot."

"Watch your backside, Tag. It's not over yet."

CHAPTER 10

"I don't like it." Cowboy stood on the dock trying to finish his lunch while he watched Tag get the boat ready. "And why are we taking Ghost?"

Tag sighed. "I've given this thing a lot of thought, and I think our best chance is to stick with our original story. We're just a couple of kids who like to dive. When we worked for Davis and Spear we didn't find anything. Now we're going on with business as usual. Just in case, I'm taking Ghost because I don't want him home alone."

The big dog barked as if in agreement and licked Tag's face.

"I still don't like it." Cowboy reluctantly stepped into the boat. "What if those guys who busted up the bait shack come after us out there?"

"Those St. David's bums don't know these reefs as well as we do. They wouldn't have a prayer if they tried to outmaneuver us." Tag started the motor and headed out across the open water.

"What are we going to do with the you-know-what in the yellow bag, which we supposedly didn't find?" Cowboy asked.

"I've thought about that too. When the coast is clear, we'll bury it somewhere on Harrington Sound Road near Devil's Hole. They'll never know what happened to it."

"I hope you're right about all this." Cowboy sat down, double-checked his tank, and tightened his weight belt.

Tag anchored behind a reef not far from Tiger Head. He was hoping that if anyone was watching they would think the boys were diving in a new place.

Tag tucked a hammer and chisel into his canvas diving bag and lifted his harness over his head. "Ready to go find that treasure?"

"Past ready. Did you bring something for the moray?"

"Thanks for reminding me." Tag reached into a box and took out two large bait fish. He held them in one hand while he pulled his face mask into place. "You behave up here, Ghost. Guard the boat until we get back." Tag gave the signal to Cowboy. "Let's do it."

Once they were in the water, the boys made straight for the hole in Tiger Head. Cowboy watched while Tag coaxed the small moray out of its hiding place with one of the bait fish.

For a moment the moray hovered in the opening, staring at them with dull, snakelike eyes. Then the green body slithered out of the hole. The fierce-looking mouth opened and closed in a steady rhythm, displaying long, sharp teeth. When it struck it moved so quickly that it caught Tag by surprise, yanking the fish from his hand. It took its prize and swam away to finish it off.

Tag made the *okay* sign with his thumb and forefinger. Cautiously he brought out the other fish and dangled it near the entrance of the hole. Like lightning a second moray grabbed one end. It rolled and spun, trying to pull the fish inside the hole, but this time Tag was ready. He held on until the moray had to come out of the hole to retrieve its prey.

Once that eel was gone, Tag went to work, hoping that would be the last of them. He took the hammer and chisel and began working to widen the hole. The reef here was thin and brittle and the work was easy. In no time he had made a hole big enough to squeeze through.

Tag unclipped his light and looked around the inside of the cave. It was large, with several dark passages leading off into other parts of the reef, and it was breathtaking. The light shimmered off the walls in myriad colors. But there was no time to stop and appreciate the beauty. They had only an hour's worth of air and the morays could decide to come back at any time.

There was no sign of the galleon. Tag hadn't

really expected that there would be. The timbers would probably be rotted by now. The best they could hope for would be artifacts.

This time both boys used Ping-Pong paddles. They dropped to their knees and delicately swept at the sand on the bottom of the cave. Tag felt a tap on his shoulder. Cowboy handed him a black lump. Tag turned it over in his hands. Whatever it had been, it had turned to silver sulfide. He motioned for Cowboy to put the lump into the orange diving bag attached to his friend's belt.

Tag continued working, waving away layers of sand deposited over centuries. Something glistened and caught his eye. Gently he pulled it up. It was a solid gold dagger. The hilt was ornate, and three large emeralds had been set in the handle. Tag clutched the dagger tightly and closed his eyes. If only his dad had lived to see this.

Cowboy tapped Tag's shoulder again. This time he held up a gold medallion. It had a cross in the center and letters on the back. Tag nodded and showed him the dagger. Cowboy's eyes danced with excitement. He grabbed Tag, picked him up off the floor of the ocean, and threw him a few feet up in the water.

Tag smiled and pointed at the gauge on his tank. They had already been down almost an hour. If they were going to keep working, they'd have to go back to the boat for more air.

When they neared the surface of the water, Tag spotted the white bottom of another boat not far from theirs. As they broke the surface they could hear Ghost barking furiously.

The other boat sped away, but not before Tag looked up into the mocking black eyes of the boy who had attacked him at the bait shack.

Ghost was whining and thrashing wildly around in a circle. Blood streamed down his right front leg.

"He's hurt!" Tag hoisted himself into the boat, yanked off his mask and tank, and rushed to examine the wound. "It's okay, Ghost," he said soothingly. "Let me take a look."

Cowboy handed him the first-aid kit. "How bad is it?"

"Could have been worse. They just grazed him with a rock or something." Tag continued to talk gently to his pet while he applied antiseptic and bandages. "They were probably going to sabotage the boat, but Ghost had other ideas."

"This is getting worse all the time, Tag. Maybe we should just give the stuff to them and get it over with."

"Right. And I guess you think they'll just pat us on the head and let us go on our way?"

Cowboy looked miserably at the floor of the boat. "I don't know what to think anymore."

Tag stroked Ghost's matted fur. "Somehow we have to figure out a plan that will get rid of the drugs and save our skins at the same time."

CHAPTER 11

The bell on the screen door tinkled softly. Tag looked around the diving shop. "Gamell? Anybody here?"

"Hang on. I'm coming." Gamell moved aside the curtain he used for a door to the back room. "Oh, it's you." The elderly man stepped behind the counter. "What can I do for you boys today?"

Tag unzipped the orange canvas bag, drew out the black lump, and set it on the counter.

Gamell adjusted his glasses and examined it. He reached under the counter for a small chisel. Carefully he cracked the lump open. It split perfectly. On the inside was an impression of a cross and what looked like a castle. "Hmmm, not bad."

"What is it?" Cowboy asked.

"It *was* silver. A piece of eight." Gamell held it up. "I can't make out the date. It's too far gone."

"Are you saying that this thing used to be a coin?" Tag leaned forward. "Was it a Spanish coin, by any chance?"

Gamell nodded. "It's not worth anything now, though. Once silver oxidizes, it's pretty much useless." He handed the pieces to Tag. "Where did you find it?"

The corners of Tag's mouth turned up mischievously. "Guess."

"Tiger Head?"

Cowboy nudged Tag's elbow. "Show him the rest of it."

"There's more?" Gamell ran his hand through his hair and sat back on a tall stool.

Tag took out the dagger and laid it gently on the counter. Gamell didn't touch it. He just stared at the golden knife, transfixed. "You found it, didn't you? You found *El Patrón*."

"We think so. But we couldn't have done it

without you. Cowboy and I have talked it over. You're a full partner in everything we find."

The old man took his handkerchief out of his pocket and wiped his eyes. "After all these years, it's finally decided to show itself."

"Actually it didn't really show itself. It's inside the reef." Tag lifted the last object out of the bag. "This medallion was down there too. Ghost had a little accident and we didn't get to search as long as we wanted, but we figure there's lots more where this came from. We'll try to go back down tomorrow."

Gamell picked up the gold medallion and fingered the crest on the front. He turned it over. On the back were the initials *B.D.C.* "This is just what you need to apply for a license to bring the rest of the stuff up. Here's proof it's definitely *El Patrón.* The admiral left his calling card. *B.D.C.*—Admiral Bartolomé de Campos. This good-luck charm must have belonged to him. Now you can have the site registered so that none of the so-called experts can steal it out from under you."

Tag zipped up the bag and slung it over his

shoulder. "Will you take care of the paper-work for us, Gamell? And, if it's all right, we'd like to keep what we've found so far in your safe. We're having a little trouble with some of the St. David's crowd right now and we don't want it to fall into the wrong hands."

"What kind of trouble? Bush?"

"Some. They hurt Ghost and they're using voodoo to try and scare us."

The old man held up his finger. "You wait here." He disappeared through the curtain. In a few moments he was back. "Here." He handed them a paper sack.

Tag looked inside and frowned. "Feathers and chicken bones?"

"I know it sounds silly, but if they really know their black magic, they'll be scared to death of these. Stick them in front of your house, boat, everywhere. They won't mess with you."

Chapter 12

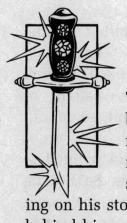

That afternoon Tag sat on the braided rug on his living room floor looking through his father's diary. Cowboy was stretched out on the sofa, sleeping on his stomach with his right arm folded behind him, snoring.

The sound of several small engines broke the silence.

"What . . . What was that?" Cowboy sat up and tried to focus.

Tag looked out the window. "It was hard to tell over all the noise you were making, but it looks like we have company."

Cowboy moved to the window. "It's the St. David's creeps."

The same three boys had driven up on old mopeds. They stopped on the other side of the feathers Tag had stuck in the ground near the house.

The leader called to them. "Hey, little man. How's your doggie?"

Tag's face turned red. He started for the door. Cowboy caught his arm. "That's what they want you to do. Don't you see? Gamell was right. Those dummies are afraid of a couple of white feathers and some old bones."

Tag slid the window open and pointed to the feathers and chicken bones he'd hung from the edge of the roof. "Hey, we've got powerful magic in here. Unless you want to wind up in your mama's stewpot tomorrow as a toad, you and your playmates better get lost."

Two of the boys stepped back toward the mopeds. The leader stood his ground. "You don't scare me, little man. You can't stay in there forever." He moved to his moped and started the motor. "We'll be waiting!"

Tag watched them ride off and dropped the curtain. "Did you make those phone calls I asked you to?"

Cowboy nodded. "I hope this works."

Tag looked at his watch. "Me too. Looks like it's time. Let's go."

CHAPTER 13

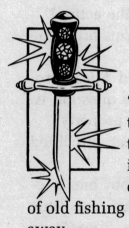

"It's getting late. Do you think they'll show?" Cowboy sat near the motor in Tag's boat, searching the water around them. The only other vessels were a couple of old fishing boats, and they were a half mile away.

"When you called, you told them we wanted to trade the drugs for five hundred dollars, didn't you?" Tag popped a peanut into his mouth.

"That's what you told me to say."

"Then don't worry. They'll show."

"You also told me to call Thomas. He said he'd be here too, but I don't see him."

"He'll be here."

From the distance a blue-and-white outboard slowly approached Tag's boat. Davis and Spear anchored next to them.

The heavyset man had an angry look on his face. "So, you two thought you'd be cute and cut yourselves in for a piece of the action?"

"Why not?" Tag shrugged. "You bring the money?"

Davis snapped his fingers and Spear produced a large wad of bills. "The question is, boys, did you bring our missing property?"

Cowboy reached under the seat and lifted up the yellow bag.

"Good!" Davis rubbed his chubby hands together. "Why don't you relieve our little friends of what is rightfully ours, Spear?"

Spear took a gun out of his shirt. "Whatever you say, Davis." Spear stepped into Tag's boat and tossed the yellow package to Davis.

Davis looked inside. "It's all here." He threw Spear some rope. "Make sure you tie them good and tight. We wouldn't want them to miss the party."

"Wait a minute!" Tag yelled as he struggled against the big man. "You were supposed to pay us."

"Oh, we're gonna pay you all right. You and your nosy friend are going to get exactly what you deserve." Davis handed a small bundle to Spear. "Set the timer for ten minutes. We don't want to be anywhere around when it goes off."

Spear tied the last knot around Tag's feet and then stuffed rags in both boys' mouths. He set the timer and climbed back into his own boat.

Davis waved at them. "Bye, boys. I know you're just *dying* for us to leave." He laughed and pointed the blue-and-white boat toward shore.

The two fishing boats Cowboy had noticed earlier had moved in. One stopped in front of the outboard. Thomas spoke to them through a megaphone. "This is the police. Throw down your weapons. I repeat, throw down your weapons."

The second fishing boat moved in beside the outboard, making escape impossible. Several rifles were trained on Davis and Spear.

Davis put his hands in the air. Spear cursed, stepped back, and pointed the gun at Tag's head. His finger started to squeeze the trigger.

Suddenly he jerked backward, dropped the pistol, and fell, clutching his bloodstained arm. The sharpshooter in the fishing boat kept his sights on Spear until Thomas stepped down into the blue-and-white boat and hand-cuffed him.

Thomas helped get the two criminals onto the fishing boat. Then he maneuvered the blue-and-white outboard close to the boys. He pulled the rag out of Tag's mouth.

"Quick, there's a bomb!" Tag motioned to the small bundle with his head.

Thomas grabbed it and looked at the timer. Thirty seconds. He flung it as far as he could out into the ocean, and, without untying the boys, he started Tag's boat and gave it full throttle.

The sea exploded behind them. Pieces of rock and coral flew into the air. A giant wave hit Tag's small boat and tossed the bow into the air. It came down hard, slapping its passengers to the bottom of the boat.

Thomas shook himself and struggled to his feet. The boys were lying on the bottom of the boat like wet rag dolls. Thomas cut Tag loose and then went to work on Cowboy. "Are you all right?"

Tag rubbed his wrists. "I think so."

Cowboy moaned and sat up. "Well, I'm not all right. Every bone in my body aches."

"We arrested Spear and Davis." Thomas tried to restart the engine. "If we're lucky they'll tell us who made the drop."

Tag wasn't listening. He was staring back toward Tiger Head. "How much damage do you think it did?"

"What, to the reef?" Thomas asked. "Plenty, I'd say. Probably collapsed the whole tail end of it."

Tag slumped. "I guess that's the end of our treasure hunting."

"What are you talking about?" Thomas finally got the engine to start. "Those crooks don't know it, but they probably just did you guys a favor. Once you clear away some of that rock, *El Patrón* will be that much easier to salvage."

"You knew?" Tag was astonished.

"Of course. Your dad and I weren't partners all those years for nothing." Thomas winked at them. "And if you guys cut me in, I might just be persuaded to help."

"What about your job? I don't think they were too happy the last time you went diving."

"After this bust, I'll be able to call the shots. The boys down at the station will probably make me chief now. What do you say?"

Tag smiled and gave him the thumbs-up sign. "I say let's go for it."

GARY PAULSEN
ADVENTURE GUIDE

DEEP-SEA DIVING

TIPS FOR SAFE DIVING

1. Be physically prepared. Don't try diving unless you exercise regularly and are a good swimmer. Get a medical checkup to be sure.

2. Enroll in a recognized training program. Just reading about diving doesn't make you a diver.

3. Make sure you have good equipment. Have it tested and checked before each dive.

4. Find out about the area you are planning to dive in. Know beforehand about any special weather or water current conditions.

5. Do not dive alone. Always take someone with you under the water, and if possible have someone waiting at the surface.

6. Know what to do in case of an emergency, and carry first-aid equipment.

7. Plan your dive and make sure all those involved stick to the plan.

8. If you discover that you have any physical abnormality before or after a dive, seek medical attention.

EQUIPMENT USED IN SCUBA DIVING

It's always a good idea to have an equipment checklist so that you don't find yourself out on the water, ready to dive but missing part of your gear.

Make sure you start with a full tank of air with a reserve valve or a submersible pressure gauge that has been double-checked for accuracy.

Your weight belt should be chosen by figuring your body's size and buoyancy—generally one pound for every ten pounds of body weight.

A face mask, snorkel, fins, flotation vest, and wet suit are basic equipment.

Don't forget your special instruments. You'll need a depth gauge, a waterproof watch and flashlight, and an underwater compass.

By the way, it's called *scuba* diving because the letters in *scuba* stand for:

> **S**elf
> **C**ontained
> **U**nderwater
> **B**reathing
> **A**pparatus

Don't miss all the exciting action!

Read the other action-packed books in Gary Paulsen's WORLD OF ADVENTURE!

The Legend of Red Horse Cavern

Will Little Bear Tucker and his friend Sarah Thompson have heard the eerie Apache legend many times. Will's grandfather especially loves to tell them about Red Horse—an Indian brave who betrayed his people, was beheaded, and now haunts the Sacramento Mountain range, searching for his head. To Will and Sarah it's just a story—until they decide to explore a newfound mountain cave, a cave filled with dangerous treasures.

Deep underground Will and Sarah uncover an old chest stuffed with a million dollars. But now armed bandits are after them. When they find a gold Apache statue hidden in a skull, it seems Red Horse is hunting them too. Then they lose their way, and each step they take in the damp, dark cavern could be their last.

Rodomonte's Revenge

Friends Brett Wilder and Tom Houston are video game whizzes. So when a new virtual reality arcade called Rodomonte's Revenge opens near their home, they make sure they're its first customers. The game is awesome. There are flaming fire rivers to jump, beastly buzz-bugs to fight, and ugly tunnel spiders to escape. If they're good enough they'll face

Rodomonte, an evil giant waiting to do battle within his hidden castle.

But soon after they play the game, strange things start happening to Brett and Tom. The computer is taking over their minds. Now everything that happens in the game is happening in real life. A buzz-bug could gnaw off their ears. Rodomonte could smash them to bits. Brett and Tom have no choice but to play Rodomonte's Revenge again. This time they'll be playing for their lives.

Escape from Fire Mountain

". . . please, anybody . . . fire . . . need help."

That's the urgent cry thirteen-year-old Nikki Roberts hears over the CB radio the weekend she's left alone in her family's hunting lodge. The message also says that the sender is trapped near a bend in the river. Nikki knows it's dangerous, but she has to try to help. She paddles her canoe downriver, coming closer to the thick black smoke of the forest fire with each stroke. When she reaches the bend, Nikki climbs onshore. There, covered with soot and huddled on a rock ledge, sit two small children.

Nikki struggles to get the children to safety. Flames roar around them. Trees splinter to the ground. But as Nikki tries to escape the fire, she doesn't know that two poachers are also hot on her trail. They fear that she and the children have seen too much of their illegal operation—and they'll do anything to keep the kids from making it back to the lodge alive.

The Rock Jockeys

Devil's Wall.

Rick Williams and his friends J.D. and Spud—the Rock Jockeys—are attempting to become the first and youngest climbers to ascend the north face of their area's most treacherous mountain. They're also out to discover if a B-17 bomber rumored to have crashed into the mountain years ago is really there.

As the Rock Jockeys explore Devil's Wall, they stumble upon the plane's battered shell. Inside, they find items that seem to have belonged to the crew, including a diary written by the navigator. Spud later falls into a deep hole and finds something even more frightening: a human skull and bones. To find out where they might have come from, the boys read the navigator's story in the diary. It reveals a gruesome secret that heightens the dangers the mountain might hold for the Rock Jockeys.

Hook 'Em, Snotty!

Bobbie Walker loves working on her grandfather's ranch. She hates the fact that her cousin Alex is coming up from Los Angeles to visit and will probably ruin her summer. Alex can barely ride a horse and doesn't know the first thing about roping. There is no way Alex can survive a ride into the flats to round up wild cattle. But Bobbie is going to have to let her tag along anyway.

Out in the flats the weather turns bad. Even worse, Bobbie knows that she'll have to watch out for the

Bledsoe boys, two mischievous brothers who are usually up to no good. When the boys rustle the girls' cattle, Bobbie and Alex team up to teach the Bledsoes a lesson. But with the wild bull Diablo on the loose, the fun and games may soon turn deadly serious.

Danger on Midnight River

Daniel Martin doesn't want to go to Camp Eagle Nest. He wants to spend the summer as he always does: with his uncle Smitty in the Rocky Mountains. Daniel is a slow learner, but most other kids call him retarded. Daniel knows that at camp, things are only going to get worse. His nightmare comes true when he and three bullies must ride the camp van together.

On the trip to camp Daniel is the butt of the bullies' jokes. He ignores them and concentrates on the roads outside. He thinks they may be lost. As the van crosses a wooden bridge, the planks suddenly give way. The van plunges into the raging river below. Daniel struggles to shore, but the driver and the other boys are nowhere to be found. It's freezing, and night is setting in. Daniel faces a difficult decision. He could save himself . . . or risk everything to try to rescue the others too.

The Gorgon Slayer

Eleven-year-old Warren Trumbull has a crazy job. He works for Prince Charming's Damsel in Distress

Rescue Agency, saving people from hideous monsters, evil warlocks, and wicked witches. One day Warren gets the most dangerous assignment of all: He must exterminate a Gorgon. Warren will need all his courage and skill—and a surprise weapon—to become a true Gorgon slayer.

Captive!

When masked gunmen storm into his classroom, Roman Sanchez and three other boys are taken hostage. They are hauled to a run-down mountain cabin, bound with rope, and given no food. With each passing hour the kidnappers' deadly threats become more real. Roman knows time is running out. He and the other boys must pull together now and launch a last desperate fight for freedom.

Project: A Perfect World

When Jim Stanton's family moves to a small town in New Mexico, everyone but Jim is happy. His dad has a great job as a research scientist at Folsum Laboratories. His mom has a beautiful new house. Folsum Labs even buys a bunch of new toys for his little sister.

But there's something strange about the town. The people all dress and act alike. Everyone's *too* polite. And they're all eerily obedient to the bosses at Folsum Labs.

Though he has been warned not to leave town, Jim wanders into the nearby mountains looking for excitement. There he meets Maria, a mountain girl with a shocking secret that involves Folsum Laboratories, a dangerous mind control experiment, and—most frightening of all—Jim's family.

Look for these thrill-packed adventures coming soon!

Skydive!

Jesse Rodriguez has a pretty exciting job for a thirteen-year-old, working for his friend Buck at a small flight and skydiving school near Seattle. But he still can't wait to turn sixteen and finally be old enough to make his first jump. Buck has been like a father to him ever since Jesse's dad died, and has made sure Jesse picks up all he needs to know about skydiving while he does odd jobs around the airport.

But Jesse and his friend Robin Waterford have also learned something very disturbing. Someone's been using the airport for an illegal transportation operation, and Jesse's worried that Buck's involved. Jesse and Robin are soon in the middle of a dangerous international situation, forced to make their first jumps sooner than they ever expected!

The Seventh Crystal

Each day at exactly three P.M., Chris Masters faces two great challenges. First he races home, trying to avoid the school bullies who have made a career of beating him up. Then, once he's safely back in his bedroom, he takes on another opponent—a computer game called The Seventh Crystal.

The high-tech game arrived mysteriously in the mail one day, without a return address or a letter from the sender. Chris doesn't even know who created it, but he does know The Seventh Crystal is the most challenging computer game he has ever faced. Chris becomes obsessed with mastering the game. So obsessed that the game seems *real*—and then Chris has something much bigger than bullies to worry about.